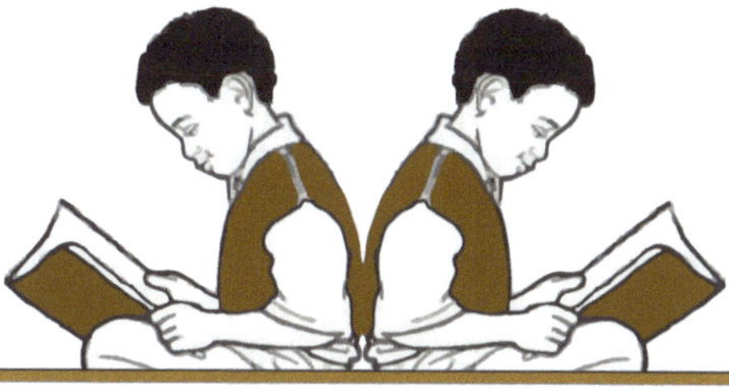

THIS BOOK BELONGS TO

Icon Publishing Limited
P. O. Box OD 972
Odorkor, Accra
Ghana
www.facebook.com/myicongh
www.twitter.com/myicongh
+233 (0)23 3505 055,

iconpublishingltd@gmail.com
iconpublishing@ymail.com
enquiries.icongh@gmail.com

Cover and Interior Design by iCON-gh +233 24 4890 432

ISBN: 978-9988-8566-5-6

THE PRINCESS WHO MARRIED THE PYTHON

AND ANOTHER TALE FROM AFRICA*

*The Married Woman with Two Lovers

Dan Odei

Kwame Insaidoo

This folktale from Ghana sought to teach young women to be careful and wary of strangers who approached them for their hands in marriage.

A lovely princess lived with her parents in the small village of Koodum. Even though she was ripe for marriage, she refused the hands of all prospective suitors in her village and the neighbouring villages. Many of the suitors praised her for her proper upbringing and her uprightness in dealing with people, but the princess refused them all, saying that she had not yet found her lover. Her parents encouraged her to pick a local man from one of the good families in Koodum and settle down with him, but she refused to listen to them. Her parents did not want her to marry a total stranger whom they knew nothing about.

One day the python heard the story of the beautiful princess in Koodum who refused to marry all the prospective suitors in the village, so he decided to change himself into a tall, dark, and handsome man to seek the princess's hand in marriage. When the disguised python reached the princess at Koodum, he saw her washing her clothes at the bank of the main river.

The princess, upon seeing the strange man, was seized with feelings of what she described as "love at first sight."

But, boy, whatever it was, she became overjoyed and swore that she had found her lover.

The handsome man greeted the princess, "Hello, my gorgeous and charming lady. How do you do?"

The princess smilingly replied, "I am not a charming and a gorgeous lady." So the man changed his greeting to "Hello, somebody's Princess Charming." To that greeting the princess replied, "I am not anybody's princess." The man switched his words to "Hello, my sweet, charming princess-to-be," to which she smilingly and pleasingly responded, "Good morning, my Prince Charming. You are the one I have been waiting for all my life. Where have you been all this time?"

The princess took the man home to meet her parents. She introduced him as the Prince Charming she had been waiting for all her life, adding, "Mom and Dad, I have finally found the soul mate that God made for me."

Her parents were not in favour of their only daughter marrying a total stranger. Her father asked the man many questions and found his answers to be unsatisfactory. The princess's mother could not determine the village the man came from and was very much against her daughter marrying him. The more the parents protested against their daughter's intention of

*Exchanges of flattery between the charming princess and the
disguised python*

marrying the man, the more forceful and belligerent their daughter became. She even threatened to kill herself if she was not allowed to marry her Prince Charming. The parents reluctantly gave up their resistance and opposition to the marriage, and the stranger married the princess in a small gathering at the king's palace.

After the marriage, the man took her beautiful bride to his hometown; but they travelled and travelled and travelled for more than three days, and still they did not reach his hometown. The princess was tired and began complaining about the long trip; indeed, she was beginning to regret her decision to marry him. But before long they came across a thick, gloomy, dark area of the bush with a big river flowing through it. The husband told his wife that they had finally reached his home. The princess was fearful of the strange environment her husband called home and began recalling her parent's advice not to marry strangers. Before she could say anything, her husband changed himself back into a huge python and moved into the thick forest at the top of the river in the deep ravine, bidding his wife to follow.

She followed him to a tiny hut made of sticks and settled in with him. Her new husband told her that he had decided to come and marry her to teach her a lesson

The husband transforming himself into a huge python

because she had been disobedient to her parents and had been arrogant and conceited toward all the village men who had sought her hand in marriage. He told her to serve him eggs and live chickens every day and warned that if she attempted to run away, he would swallow her whole.

The following day, when the python went to hunt for food with his fellow pythons, the princess sat down near a hill and began to sob. As she sobbed, she sang a sorrowful song:

Hello, my parents
All your advice about strangers was right
The stranger I married was not a man, but a python
And if you don't send someone to rescue me
He will soon swallow me

Whenever her husband went to work, she sang her song. This continued for over two years, and she grew very lean like a skeleton. Her parents had also been frantically searching for her for all those years but had not been successful.

One morning when the princess was sobbing and singing her mournful song, a parrot heard the sad song and saw the princess and reported what she heard and saw to the girl's parents. Her parents rapidly organized the villagers of Koodum to find the princess, with the parrot leading the way. When the parents reached the river and saw that their daughter's husband was a python, they hid in the bushes because they were afraid of him. But when he went to work the next day, they seized the princess and ran away with her.

As fate would have it, the python decided to cut his work short for the day because all his friends had house chores to do for the rest of the day. When he got home, he could not find his wife. He searched all around the neighbouring bushes and huts but could not find her, so he decided to follow the path back to the princess's village.

The python moved as swiftly as he could and eventually spotted his wife running with her parents and the villagers back to Koodum. The python vowed to kill the parents to get his wife back. He made a mad dash to reach her, but he fell into a large hill filled with millions of big red ants, who trapped him for their meal. He swallowed more ants than he could digest, and so the ants choked him to death. The villagers of Koodum rushed to the anthill, chopped the python into little pieces, and threw them all over the village.

This story reminds us of the ancient days in many parts of Africa, when parents did not want their daughters to marry strangers. They arranged most of the marriages; but, as could be expected; many young girls rebelled against such practices. Many societies narrated such fearful stories to frighten rebellious young women into accepting these arranged marriages. The elders employed such stories to educate young women to be cautious of strangers and not to just marry any stranger they met willy-nilly.

Even though many girls objected to such arranged marriages, the folktales were designed to advise and educate men and women in general to be cautious of the partners they selected for such an important institution and lifelong commitment as marriage. These folktales and others like it were employed to caution would-be wives and husbands to take their time to find out more information about their prospective partners such as: what family had raised them, whether the family had a history of drug or alcohol use, what kinds of diseases the family had, the family's history, whether the prospective partner had adequately prepared himself to be a provider, and the sexual morality of the prospective partner (Was she a woman of easy virtue? Was he a womanizer?). These critical questions were taught to the impressionable young girls and boys through these folktales.

Answer the following questions:

1.   What was the name of the village in which the princess lived?

2.   What did all the suitors praise the princess for?

3.   What did the python decide to do when he heard that the princess had turned down the marriage offers from the various suitors?

4.   What did the princess threaten to do if her parents did not allow her to marry her 'Prince Charming'?

5.   What did the python man say were his reasons for coming to marry the princess?

6.   What was the warning the python man gave the princess after he had revealed his true identity?

7. Give synonyms for the following words as they have been used in the story,
    a. gorgeous — (paragraph 4)
    b. reluctantly — (paragraph 7)
    c. beautiful — (paragraph 8)
    d. tired — (paragraph 8)
    e. began — (paragraph 8)
    f. arrogant — (paragraph 9
    g. rapidly — (paragraph 12)

8. Which of the following would be the best alternative title of the story?
    a. Determination leads to success
    b. It pays to wait
    c. The importance of faithfulness
    d. The consequences of disobedience.

The Married Woman With Two Lovers

This folktale from the Gambia tells about a perverted married woman with two lovers.

Penda, the most beautiful woman in the village of Sando, was married to the most famous wrestler in the whole community. Penda had two other lovers that she had been in love with ever since her wedding day. She called both lovers her sugar daddies. Her husband was suspicious of her interactions with those other men, but Penda was so cunning and deceitful that she was able to twist her husband around her little finger so that he could find no concrete evidence of her infidelity.

One day the husband decided to find out if his wife was indeed cheating on him, so he concocted a simple plan. He told his wife that his next wrestling match would take him to another town about two hundred miles away in Sotokoba and that he would not be back until dusk the next day. The wife saw her husband off in a lorry station; but, unbeknownst to her, as soon as the lorry took off he instructed the driver to take him in a loop to his next-door neighbour's house where he could keep an eye on his house to find out if the wife had any so-called sugar daddies.

The wife was absolutely convinced that her husband had gone to the town of Sotokoba to wrestle with the best wrestlers there. Since she had personally seen him off at the lorry station, she felt safe to send for both of her lovers to come to her house at different times: she wanted the richest lover to be the first to come to her, while the other lover should come by at midnight.

Before nightfall, the rich sugar daddy arrived at her house, entered into her sitting room, and began drinking palm wine, the local gin, and all sorts of sumptuous food that she had meticulously prepared for him. She had decorated the kitchen table with all sorts of flowers, from hibiscus to red roses, and set the table with two glasses, two sets of cutlery, and two plates. Indeed everything on the table was in pairs especially set for the couple to enjoy. They sat up at the kitchen table drinking and feasting on the delicious meals Penda had prepared, until they retired to the bedroom to make love.

The moment they entered the bedroom, they heard footsteps at the back door of the house. The wife instinctively knew that it was her husband, and she knew she would be in trouble after being caught red-handed in her shenanigans. She was fretting and thinking hard about what to do to avert the impending disaster, which could lead to her death or a bitter divorce or the sudden death of her lover. As she was desperately thinking of what to do, she saw an empty pot in the doorway and asked her sugar daddy to quickly hide inside it. When he entered the pot, the woman covered it with a big leaf, and at the same time her husband opened the door and headed straight into the bedroom.

When the husband saw that his wife was naked, he became suspicious that she was with another man. But his wife explained that she was naked because the room was too hot for her. Thereupon, the husband retorted, "You smell musty like you have been having sex."

The wife replied, "Hey, fool, you have a lot to learn about us women! Don't you know that when it is hot like this, it is natural for women to smell musty like nature intended for us to be?"

When the husband went to the kitchen and saw the meticulous arrangements of pairs of cutlery, plates, cups, and napkins, he demanded to know whom they were for. The wife replied that she was practising the way celebrities decorated their homes for grand and auspicious occasions, "so my husband will one day be honoured to sit at the head of the table." Her husband

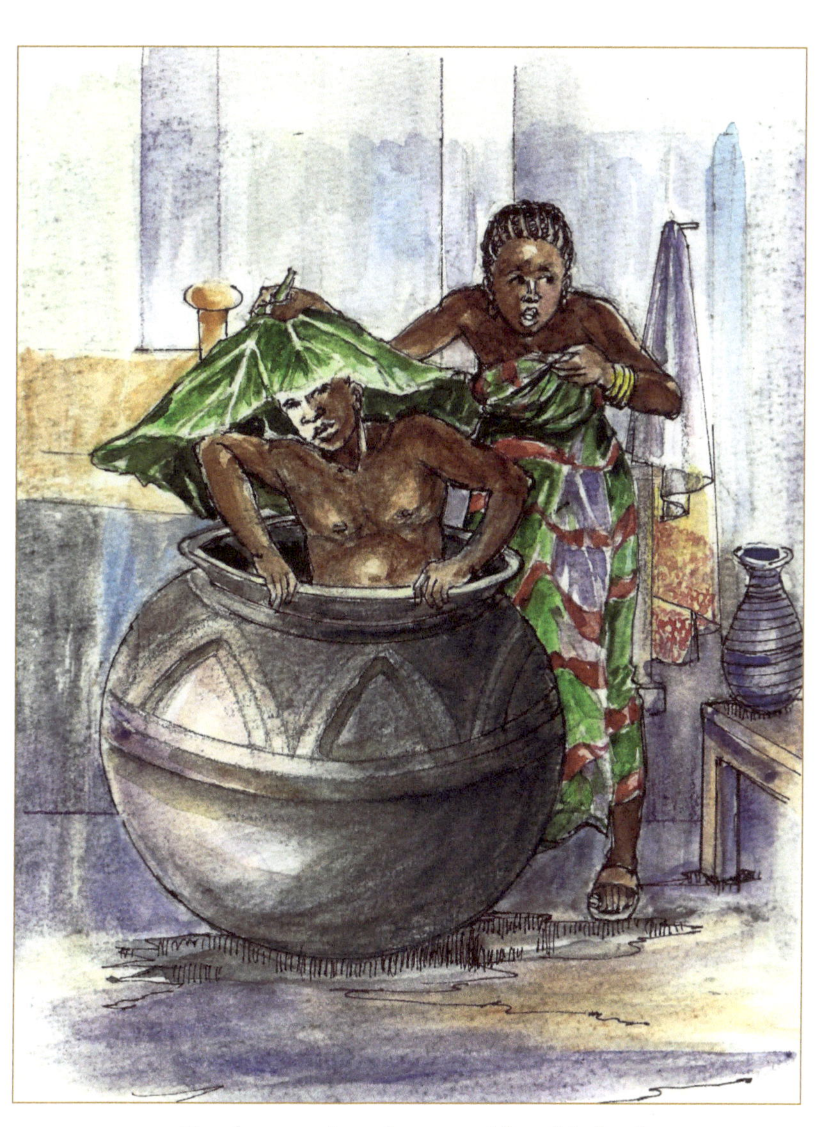

Penda covering the pot with a big leaf

became happy that she was thinking highly of him by imagining him as the leader of a big occasion.

The husband replied, "Oh, if you think highly of me, I will make you even more proud. I am going to fight hard and conquer the best wrestlers in the whole nation so you can bring your dream of honouring me to reality."

Meanwhile, it was midnight, and the other sugar daddy was at her doorstep, knocking at her door and demanding to get inside because it was his turn to make love to Penda. She thought hard and then opened the door and politely asked her lover, "Oh, what took you so long to come for the pot? My uncle is desperately waiting for the pot to fill it with his wine for market early tomorrow. He is anxiously waiting for you." She turned to her husband who was standing behind her and said, "My uncle sent for him early during the day, but the fool took so long to come and fetch this precious pot and made my poor uncle wait all day long for it."

Penda's lover understood what was going on and quietly lifted the big pot onto his head. But before he left, Penda told him to take good care of the pot, explaining, "It contains my precious sugar." The husband and his wife returned to her bed while her sugar daddy went away with the big pot on his head.

The sugar daddy carrying the big pot on his head

The sugar daddy had walked for about two miles, still carrying the big pot on his head, when all of a sudden he heard a voice from the pot. The man thought that the sugar in the pot had begun to melt. The man in the pot shouted, "Hey, fella! Let me down. I am crammed in, and it's hot in here, and I need some air."

When the man put the pot down, the lover in the pot jumped out and was surprised to see the other lover. The second lover asked him what he was doing in the pot. He answered, "Aren't you lucky I saved you from the woman's husband?" The lovers began to argue. The second lover argued that since he had taken the pot out of the house, he was the true hero, while the other lover replied that if the pot had not been in the bedroom, the woman's husband would have found out that he was his wife's lover and would have killed him. They stopped arguing but left their message of wisdom to men to be careful of women, particularly the married ones. They agreed that they should "fear woman and live long" and that it was dangerous for married women to fool around on their husbands because it could cost the lives of both the couples and the lovers.

Moral Lessons

The real lesson here is not only about women being unfaithful to their husbands; it is that both men and women should learn to respect the sanctity of the institution of marriage and stick to the commitments and vows they make to their spouses during the wedding ceremony. The irony of the situation is that fooling around while in marriage—while intended for pleasure—can bring unpleasant consequence to both partners, particularly the cheating partner, who may lose all respect among his or her neighbours and peers and may be scarred for the rest of his or her life.

Answer the following questions:

1.   What was the name of the beautiful woman in the story and in which town did she live?

2.   How did she refer to her two lovers?

3.   How did her husband sought to find out if his wife was cheating on him?

4.   In which town did her husband say he was going to fight the wrestling match?

5.   Why was the beautiful woman so sure that she could bring her two lovers without any problem?

6.   At which point did the woman hear footsteps at the backdoor of the house?

7.

Penda's lover understood what was going on and quietly lifted the big pot onto his head. But before he left, Penda told him to take good care of the pot, explaining, "It contains my precious sugar." The husband and his wife returned to her bed while her sugar daddy went away with the big pot on his head.

How would you describe the character of the woman and her lover as shown in the box above. Give reasons for the answer.

8. What is the most important thing you have learnt from this story?

9. What is the meaning of the expression "to be caught red-handed"?

10. Which of the following best describes Penda?
    a. fair
    b. decent
    c. unfaithful
    d. hardworking

11. List all the nouns in the first paragraph and state what type each noun is.

12. Which words could have been used to replace each of the following words in the story?
    a. beautiful — (paragraph one)
    b. famous — (paragraph one)
    c. infidelity — (paragraph one)
    d. instructed — (paragraph two)
    e. sumptuous — (paragraph four)
    f. surprised — (paragraph thirteen)

Answer the questions here.